Special Memo from

The Federation of Fright

It has come to our attention that human children have run out of nightmares. It appears that children are no longer having bad dreams, and this has led the Secret Committee for the Advancement of Real Evil (S.C.A.R.E.) to conclude that not enough things are going bump in the night.

As part of our new "Focus on Fear" campaign we have decided to hold a competition to find the Grisliest Ghoul. We will be studying the diary entries of each competitor in order to judge them on their terror tactics. The winner will be the proud owner of the famous Poisoned Chalice and will be presented with the Monster Medal.

Anyone wishing to enter should send a diary entry to the Federation of Fright by midnight on Monday.

Yours sincerely,

Z. Ombie

Zacharias Ombie (Head of Horror)

Monday 19 May

9   *Rust the chains.*

10   *Singing class. (Ask teacher to correct my "boos!"*
11   *and "oohs!" because people are laughing, instead of shaking with fear!)*

12   *Grave Owners' Association meeting at Cemetery.*
13   *Agenda—discuss raising money to buy glasses for Dracula, who keeps going to bed in other*
14   *people's coffins.*

15   *Buy more pretty sheets for the kids.*

16   *Remember to pick up clean sheets from the cleaners!*

17

18   *The Ghost*

Wednesday

8:00	-chop onions
9:00	-watch TV
10:00	-Read the newspaper
11:00	-Have a good cry
12:00	-chop more onions
13:00	-watch the news
:00	-chop onions again
00	-Go out to cry

The cry Baby

24

08 Shave

09 Shave

10 Shave

11 Shave

12 Shave

13 Shave

14 Shave

15 Shave

16 Shave

17 Shave

18 Shave

19 Shave

20

25

08 order pizza

09 Eat ~~little girl~~
10 pizza

11

12 Yummy!

13 Realize that
14 I'm covered
in hair again!

15

16 Meet up with
the cry baby

17

18 Go out to cry
... or howl

19 The werewolf

20

26

08

09

10

11

12

30	60	90	120	150	1
26/	25/8	24/9	24/10	23/11	2

	60	90	120	150	180
27/	26/8	9	25/10	24/11	24/12

	1	2	3	4	5	6
7	8	9	10	11	12	13
14	15	16	17	18	19	20
21	22	23	24	25	26	27
28	29	30				

8:00	- Ski
	- Prepare a glass of ice and ice (must not use too much ice because it gives me a headache)
9:00	- Go out hunting for a human and put him in the freezer
10:00	- Ski more (I really love it)
	- Watch TV, freezing the image all the time
11:00	- Talk to other sasquatches coldly
12:00	- Air out the igloo
13:00	- Look for the person who gave me an electric heater for my last birthday and tell him off (I bet it was Dracula—will send him some sun cream to see how he likes bad jokes)
00	- Hibernate for a while
	- See if I can borrow Werewolf's razor—I'd like an image change
	- Buy a coat (it might be cold without any fur)

The Abominable Snowman

1	2	3	4	5	6	7
8	9	10	11	12	13	14
5	16	17	18	19	20	21
2	24	25	26	27	28	

20:00 Get alarm clock repaired—it keeps ringing early and I get up in daylight (there is nothing worse for a vampire's skin than sunlight and I can't

21:00 face going to the beauty parlor and listening to Frankie complaining about the schoolkids again).

22:00 Pick up cape at the cleaners—make sure they don't give me the Ghost's sheet again. (I'm in enough

23:00 trouble with the Grave Owners' Association.)

24:00 Moonbathe—I don't think this sun cream some person sent me will be any use . . .

1:00 Sharpen teeth—the years have worn them out.

2:00 Go out for a night on the town! Go dancing, drink some tomato juice, meet new people,

3:00 watch a good horror film—but one with no vampires (I'm a little scared of them).

4:00 Get back to the cemetery—make sure I lie down in the right coffin; the other grave owners are getting annoyed.

5:00

Dracula

85 g

1	2	3	4	5	6	7
8	9	10	11	12	13	14
15	16	17	18	19	20	21
22	23	24	25	26	27	28
29	30	31				

Wednesday 2nd

January

Buy 500 feet of bandages at the drug store—these ones are getting a little dusty.

Ask Frankie, Werewolf, the Crazy Scientist, and the Ghost to help me change my bandages.

Talk about the old days (must remember NOT to invite Cry Baby—he is always crying, and we can't hear each other over his wailing).

Get back to the museum—avoid the security guards!

Call Daddy!

The Mummy

jueves
quinta
thursday

7

septiembre
setembro
september

8.00   Wake up / **No, sleep for longer.**

8.30

9.00   Go out for a run / **I said sleep for longer!**
        At the most, read the newspaper in bed.

9.30

10.00   Watch the news / **Watch cartoons.**

10.30

11.00   Take a nap / **Ha! You should have slept until later!**

11.30   **Now I feel like going out for a run.**

12.00

12.30   Go out with my girlfriend / **Go out with MY girlfriend.**

13.00

13.30   Call the Crazy Scientist to separate me from this bore! /

14.00   **Finally, we agree about something. But you're the bore.**

14.30   Write a letter to the Grave Owners' Association about

15.00   the "Two heads are better than one" graffiti at the

15.30   graveyard / **How offensive! That certainly isn't true!**

16.00   Sleep / **Oh, yeah, right. You mean snore, more like it!**

16.30

                        The **Two-**Headed **Man**

18.00

✘   Look for glasses

✘   Give Ghost a lesson in "boos"—if I can do it, surely he can!?

✔ Cancel appointment with the barber that some clever person pretending to be me made. Must have been the Snowman. Let's see how he feels when I give him an electric heater for his birthday!

✔   Ask Dracula whether he has seen my glasses (he keeps taking them by mistake)

✔   Speak to the Two-Headed Man. I'm sure I remember him saying he had one head too many ...

✔   Ask the Crazy Scientist whether he used my glasses to invent anything. He always does the same thing, and the only thing he does well is to do things wrong.

✘   Buy ointment for bruises—walking around without seeing can be VERY painful.

✔ Go to the doctor and ask why I am always looking for my glasses. Is there something I'm not facing up to?

The Headless Man

9:00 AM: PLAY SOME TRICKS ON PILOTS AND AIR TRAFFIC CONTROLLERS BY WHIZZING AROUND IN THE SKY AND THEN DISAPPEARING.

11:00 AM: FIX SUPERBRIGHT LIGHT AND COME UP WITH AN INTERESTING TECHNO TUNE TO LAND TO. WELL, YOU HAVE TO MAKE AN ENTRANCE!

2:00 PM: ABDUCT A FEW EARTHLINGS AND TRY OUT OUR NEW EAR PROBE EQUIPMENT.

3:00 PM: GO SIGHTSEEING. TRY AND CATCH THE NEWS FROM BACK HOME (WHICH IS 1,500,354,000,000,000,000,000,000,000,000.003 LIGHT YEARS AWAY).

6:00 PM: SHOW UP AT THE BARBERSHOP TO LAUGH AT THE HEADLESS MAN. I BET HE THINKS IT WAS THE SNOWMAN WHO MADE THAT APPOINTMENT!

7:00 PM: CONQUER THE WORLD.

ALIEN INVADERS

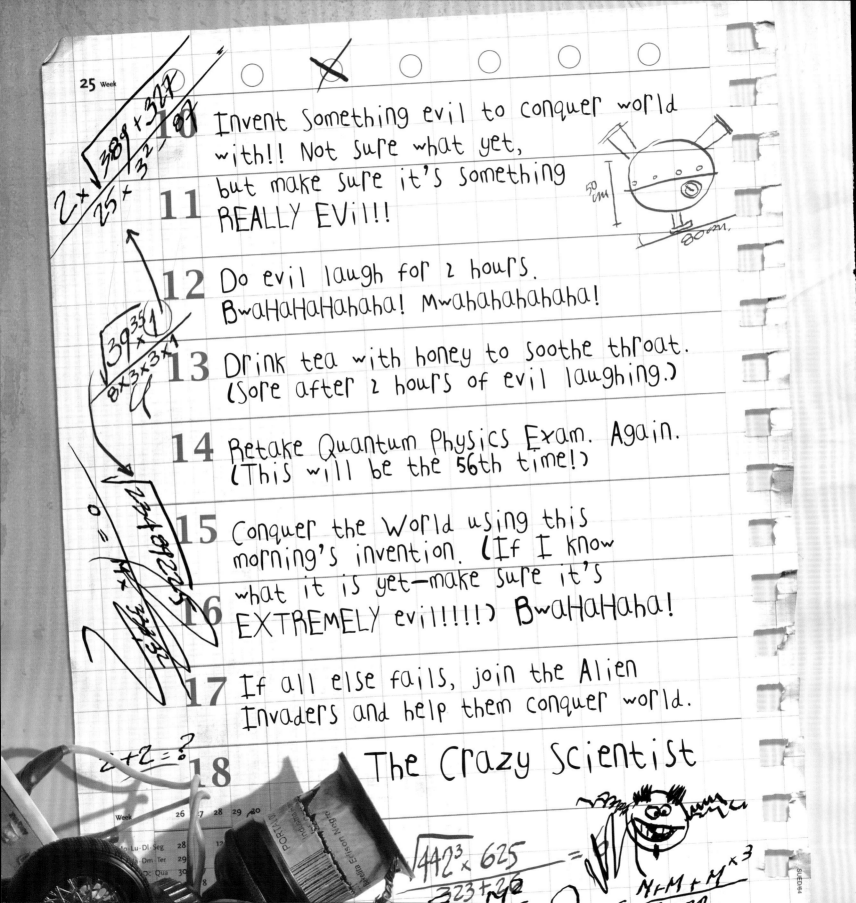

10 Invent Something evil to conquer world
with!! Not Sure what yet,

11 but make Sure it's Something
REALLY EVil!!

12 Do evil laugh for 2 hours.
BwaHaHaHaHaha! Mwahahahahaha!

13 Drink tea with honey to soothe throat.
(Sore after 2 hours of evil laughing.)

14 Retake Quantum Physics Exam. Again.
(This will be the 56th time!)

15 Conquer the World using this
morning's invention. (If I know

16 what it is yet—make Sure it's
EXTREMELY evil!!!!!) BwaHaHaha!

17 If all else fails, join the Alien
Invaders and help them conquer world.

18 The Crazy Scientist

22 23 24 25 26
29 30 31

Friday

10:00 Confirm my attendance at the 27,856ᵗʰ annual Convention of Witches. This year's topic is "Wizards and Sorcerers. Why?".

11:00 Remind the Alien Invaders they MUST respect the Skyway Code.

Invite the girls to dinner.

12:00

Go to the store and buy leech tea, skimmed cockroach wings, seagull cavities, elephant forget-me-nots, swamp mud, deadly

13:00 nightshade (I haven't seen mine since the Crazy Scientist came for coffee), polished shadows, toilet paper, cell phone prepaid

14:00 card, and gas for the broomstick.

Turn myself into a bear to carry all of this home.

:00

6:00

17:00

:00

19:00

Scrambled Frogs

Ingredients (for 4 witches):
4 serpent eggs
1 teaspoon of haunted swamp
1 teaspoon of stories that terrify at night
3 chopped cheeses
1 teaspoon of salt
8 pounds of butter

1. Wise woman of the forests, beat, but only slightly, the serpent eggs and mix with the swamp, the stories that terrify at night, the salt, and the chopped cheese.

2. Oh, Witch, you who scare everyone, put into the microwave for two minutes, generously covered with the eight pounds of butter.

3. You, who know so much, take it out and beat thoroughly. If it is not disgusting enough, put it back in for a while. If, after all of this, the consistency is still not right, then, oh, Witch of the night, who really, really, really should know better ... cook something else, since you are obviously hopeless at this.

Ask the girls why this is called scrambled frogs—it doesn't even have frogs in it!

The Witch

Thank you for entering the
Grisliest Ghoul Competition.

And the winner is ...